THE GOLDEN GIRLS

'TWAS THE NIGHT BEFORE CHRISTMAS

This is for the Girls: Betty, Bea, Rue, and Estelle, who have kept us
laughing for as long as we can remember—FS & DY

Chloe, Hillary, Nicole, and Kara . . . my favorite people to sit at a bar with every
Sunday morning, watching Golden Girls and eating waffles—AF

PENGUIN WORKSHOP
Penguin Young Readers Group
An Imprint of Penguin Random House LLC

Penguin supports copyright. Copyright fuels creativity, encourages diverse voices, promotes free speech, and creates
a vibrant culture. Thank you for buying an authorized edition of this book and for complying with copyright laws by not
reproducing, scanning, or distributing any part of it in any form without permission. You are supporting writers
and allowing Penguin to continue to publish books for every reader.

ISBN 9781524789923

10 9 8 7 6 5 4 3 2 1

THE GOLDEN GIRLS

'TWAS THE NIGHT BEFORE CHRISTMAS

BY **FRANCESCO SEDITA** AND **DOUGLAS YACKA**

ILLUSTRATED BY **ALEX FINE**

PENGUIN WORKSHOP

An Imprint of Penguin Random House

'Twas the night before Christmas
And on Richmond Street,
Three girls decked the halls,
And they made each room neat.

Their children and siblings were soon to be there.
Ma finished her famous lasagna with care.

But a storm was a-comin',
A hurricane nigh!
The planes heading in
Were unable to fly.

Outside the wind howled.
A tree snapped a branch.
Rose looked up in alarm,
"Holy cow, where is Blanche?!"

Across town, the men whooped,
And they whistled to thank her,
As Blanche jingled her bells
At the old Rusty Anchor.

While Ma in her sweatshirt and Dorothy in a vest
Had just settled down for a much-needed rest.
Rose, snug with her teddy bear, laid down her head,
While visions of St. Olaf danced in her head.

All at once, through the rain came a curious sight,

A round silhouette in the full moon's pale light.

And from the porch came the voice of a man.

The girls winced as they heard him say,

"Hi, it's me, Stan."

He was dressed up like Santa,
But ragged and droopy.
He'd lost all his money
On fake reindeer poopy.

His tale of woe made dear Rose start to cry,

While Dorothy grimaced and gave the side-eye.

After years spent with Stanley, she knew in a flash,

The only holiday gift that he wanted was cash.

Sophia cut in with a long-winded story.

"Picture it: Sicily, the year 1940."

Something about a goat, linguine, and theft.

Whatever it meant, it worked! Stan quickly left.

A moment later Blanche whirled
through the front door.
She was wet, she was cold,
she was dressed like a . . . uh . . . elf.
Rose explained that their families
simply couldn't get there.
"It's just rain!" Blanche lamented.
"How rude, I declare!"

So into the kitchen the four girls paraded,

Feeling down and depressed.

The fridge quickly was raided.

There were cookies and ice cream,

hot cocoa to make.

A salami or two, and three types of cheesecake.

For hours the girls talked,

And they laughed, and they shared.

It's likely a few flashback episodes aired.

Then suddenly, like a true holiday spell,

The girls realized they were all family as well.

You could hear them exclaim
as the day came to an end,
"Merry Christmas!
And thank you for being a friend!"